# BOPPER'S PROGRESS

# BOPPER'S PROGRESS

John Manderino

**WUNDOR**

*Editions*

First published in Great Britain in 2018 by Wundor Editions

Wundor Editions Ltd, 35B Fitzjohn's Avenue, London NW3 5JY

www.wundoreditions.com

Book Design – Matthew Smith

ISBN 978-0-9956541-8-1

Printed and bound in Great Britain by TJ International Ltd

O snail
climb Mt. Fuji
but slowly, slowly!

– Issa

*Schedule: Monday, November 8, 1981*

4:15   Wake-up

5:00   Meditation

6:30   Morning Service

7:00   Formal Breakfast

7:35   Body Practice

9:00   Work Practice

12:00  Lunch

1:00   Art Practice

3:00   Work Practice

5:00   Meditation

6:00   Light Supper

7:30   Meditation/Dokusan

9:00   Evening Service

9:45   Lights Out

WAKE-UP

## the greatest of all mistakes

Meredith is looking me dead in the eye as she does a slow dirty dance in just her little tennis skirt, using her racket in suggestive ways. She opens her mouth, about to say *Oh Bopper I want you back*, but out comes the buzzing of Raza's alarm clock.

He's in the bed next to mine. 'Razor' we call him. He's from India, a professor over there, pretty smug about it. After slapping off the alarm he makes a few smacking sounds with his mouth and gets up with a small groan. I can't see him in the dark but I know he's wearing shiny red pajamas buttoned to the throat. He turns on his flashlight and with his free hand makes his bed, which looks barely *un*made. The guy must sleep like Dracula.

And now the other one in the cabin, beachboy Nathaniel from San Diego, gets up from the bed to my other side and starts kicking around the floor at his clothes and cassettes and candy cartons, muttering 'Wait...wait,' finding his pants and boots in time to yank them on and follow Razor's flashlight out the door.

I hear their feet on the gravel path to the bathhouse.

*Get up*, I tell myself. *Count of three. Here we go. One...two... three.*

I try the other way: *Three...two...one.*

I toss off the covers and sit on the edge of the bed, arms folded against the cold. This is ridiculous. I lean to my left and fart hard. Did *Buddha* get up at four-fifteen in the morning? I kindly doubt it.

*Move.*

Searching in the dark for my flashlight, sweeping my arm all over the bed, I'm thinking I need a flashlight to find it, and one to find that one, and so on. There's a Zen saying: *Seeking the mind with the mind—is this not the greatest of all mistakes?*

I should get back into bed and ponder that, just for a minute.

By the time I get to the dimly-lit bathhouse, Razor is out of the shower flossing his perfect teeth at the sink, Nathaniel sitting on the toilet, head hung, possibly asleep. I stand over the other toilet to pee, without looking down. These are compost toilets. They don't flush. I hate that.

Another thing I avoid looking at is the mirror while I brush my teeth, knowing what that face will be wondering:

*What the hell are you doing here?*

**what the hell i'm doing here**

Meredith had this tennis instructor named Lance–his actual
name–who kept giving her books: the Zen of this, the Zen of
that. In fact, Lance himself was writing a book.

'Let me guess. About the Zen of tennis.'

'He already has a title: Don't Hit the Ball, Hit the Ball.'

'He sounds kind of silly, your Lance. Is that really his name,
by the way?'

'Wait, *you're* making fun of someone's *name?*'

Here's the note she left me:

*Bopper*

*I'm sorry but I need to be with Lance.*
*He's taught me so much more than*
*tennis, he's taught me who I am!*

*—M*

*P.S. I'm leaving you my Zen books*
*—read them.*

I began sitting every night in this sticky little country-
western bar I found, feeling sorry for myself. I enjoyed that,
especially with the right music, Patsy Cline for example:

*I...fall...to pieces...*

Sometimes I would even pull out my wallet and show
Meredith's picture to someone at the next stool: *See this*
*woman? Isn't she beautiful? Her name's Meredith. We were so*
*happy together. Then, know what she did? You ready for this?*

*Where you going?*

But I was a shift manager at a Pizza Hut up in Rogers Park, north of Chicago, a horrible job to be hungover at—all those pizzas and people. I thought about finding other work but decided it made better sense to quit drinking. So I did, I quit. I stayed home at night and watched television: *The Rockford Files, Trapper John MD, Charlie's Angels...*

But then one night after turning it off I kept lying there staring at my reflection in the blank screen: this long scrawny guy sprawled out on a couch, size elevens up on the coffee table, a family-sized bag of corn chips on his stomach.

*Jesus,* I thought.

So after that, instead of lying on the couch every night watching television, I started lying there reading from this shitload of Zen books Meredith left. I didn't know Zen from Zulu but I figured I could be just as goddam spiritual as her—or her guru loverboy Lance for that matter—any day. Hell, I was an *altar* boy for two years, and a good one too. I remember Father Crowley complimenting me on my recitation of the Confiteor: 'Very crisp,' he said. 'Very clear.'

The first book I read seemed a good place to start: *Zen Mind, Beginner's Mind,* by this actual Japanese Zen Master, Shunryu Suzuki. There was a picture of him on the back. He looked like a real nice guy. The book didn't talk much, though, about how to get spiritual. Mostly it talked about getting *rid* of stuff, including stuff like trying to get spiritual, in fact especially stuff like that.

He kept referring to my True Nature.

Which was something *all* the books talked about, as it turned out. And this True Nature of mine was my Buddha Nature, Buddha being this guy who lived in India twenty-five hundred years ago who sat under a tree one day and didn't get up again until he attained enlightenment, a state of mind I imagined to be something like the time I almost drowned in Lake Michigan—the way I felt afterwards, I mean.

I actually *intended* to drown, I'm ashamed to say. It was over a girl–what else?–another one who dumped me. This was high school, senior year, class of '73, eight years ago now. Charlotte Leclaire. Isn't that a pretty name? And what a pretty girl. And so sweet. I was nuts about her. And for a while she felt the same way, or similar, I know she did. But then I got clingy, which I tend to do:

'You're smothering me, Bopper. I can't breathe. I want out.'

After that, seeing her in the hall between classes talking to other guys—breathing freely, smiling away—I couldn't stand it. It hurt so bad I couldn't stand it.

So one muggy Saturday near the end of the school year I took the IC train downtown, walked to the Oak Street Beach, found a spot on the crowded sand and laid there on my towel, in my trunks, staring up at a fat white cloud, trying to get up the nerve. After a while I stood and walked to the water. Gazing straight ahead I made my way through all the noisy happy humans till the lake was up to my chin, then started swimming straight out. I'm not a very good swimmer but I kept going, kept going. Then all of a sudden I thought to myself *What the fuck are you doing?* and turned around. But by then I was out pretty far. I told myself not to panic—*Do! Not! Panic!*—like a loudspeaker in an air raid, and I panicked, kicking and chopping away until I was quickly limp and going under, into cloudy green silence, the water not wishing to kill me or giving a shit if it did, and I wrestled my way to the surface, got my head out, and in this deep sincere voice I never heard on me before I said, 'Help.' But the people playing in the happy shallows didn't hear and I went under again—*Jesus please I love you get me out of this*—and fought my way once more into air and sounds, one gulp and a glimpse of that fat white cloud, then under again and this time for good, I was certain, nothing left in my arms and legs. I felt sorry for my mom.

But somebody, obviously, got me. Somebody saw me and swam over, grabbed me with a burly arm, hauled me up and dragged me in like a six-foot two-inch length of seaweed. Turned out, he wasn't even a lifeguard, just a muscle-bound, crew-cutted hero, whose big meaty hand I couldn't stop shaking:

'*Thank you, thank you, thank you!*'

'You bet.'

'*You saved my life!*'

'I know.'

'*Thank you, thank you—*'

'Let go my hand, okay?'

Heading back to my towel, I nodded and smiled around at everyone, holding up my thumb. And for the rest of the day, the rest of that afternoon anyway, lying there on my towel, gazing straight up at that fat white cloud which I thought would be the last thing I ever saw, you cannot imagine how happy I felt, breathing in and breathing out, wanting nothing, needing nothing, loving this world and everyone in it with all my heart.

I kept that feeling all the way back on the train, loving my fellow passengers. But when I got home my mother's bossy new boyfriend Jerry was there, in the backyard cooking hot dogs on the grill, in his shorts and flip-flops and Hawaiian shirt, wraparound sunglasses up on his forehead. He held up a hot dog in the tongs of a long fork and told me to grab a bun.

So that was it for loving everyone in the world.

Anyway, whenever the Zen books mentioned enlightenment, that's what I imagined, the way I felt while lying on my towel on Oak Street Beach after being saved. That was my True Nature, my Buddha Nature. And Buddha was still down there. He could barely breathe under all the ugly, useless, piled-up junk of my *Un*true Nature, but he was there, if I could get to him.

I ended up reading the whole Zen collection Meredith left me, then started hitting bookstores for more. I was hooked. It was thrilling reading things like:

*At that moment, he suddenly attained Full Awakening.*

And yet I couldn't honestly say I felt any real difference in myself, any kind of awakening, full or partial. This idea that my True Nature was the same as Buddha's—well, that was a nice thought, but when I finished each book it always turned out to be just another Zen book I had read, and I would stuff it in the shelf with the others and go buy another one.

I stank of Zen. That's what you say about someone who only reads about it. *He stinks of Zen.* Which of course was something I had read.

Once in a blue moon I'd sit on the floor, straddling a pillow, cup my hands in my lap, and try meditating, try actually *doing* some Zen. But sitting there was uncomfortable and frustrating and dull. I much preferred lying on the couch reading things like, *The wild geese do not intend to cast their reflection; the water has no mind to receive their image.* Pondering that, with my corn chips.

Then one night I was looking through this expensive Buddhist monthly magazine I'd bought. In the back pages were all these ads for mats and cushions, meditationwear and incense burners—and an ad for *this* place.

'Rigorous and authentic,' it said.

*That's good, I like that,* I thought. *That's what I need.*

'On a 230-acre forested property in the Catskill Mountains of upstate New York.'

*Sounds nice.*

But the thing that *really* sold me was this picture they had of the Abbot here, of his face. What a face. A phrase from my reading came to me: *cheerfully serene.*

I wanted a face like that.

There was a phone number.

## under all these stars

Our cabin is on a high hill a couple hundred yards from the main building, a dirt and gravel path leading down with a single shaky handrail. With my flashlight I can see Razor all the way down the hill already, heading towards the main building, with that poker-up-his-butt way of walking he has. Above me the sky is so full of stars it looks *smeared* with them. I tell myself how wonderful this is, to be walking down a wooded hillside in the Catskill Mountains under all those stars, although I'd still rather be back in bed under all those covers.

'Bopper!'

I stop and wait for Nathaniel. He lost his flashlight a couple of days ago, so he's been using me and Razor to get around in the dark. I shine my light in front of his feet and he comes down carefully, holding the rail with both hands. Arriving, he starts in about the path. 'Fuckin' guy could break his—'

'Shh,' I tell him. There's silence this morning till ten.

He tells me don't be shushing him. He's very touchy, Nathaniel. He's from southern California with a long blond ponytail so you expect him to be all groovy and mellow, but he's actually a very irritable guy.

I start heading down again, Nathaniel close at my heels. Through the trees now I can make out the dark shape of the main building, a large cross above the entrance—this used to be a *Franciscan* monastery and the Zen people left it up, maybe as a way of saying it's okay to be a Christian Buddhist, or a Buddhist Christian. Meanwhile Nathaniel goes right on breaking the silence rule, telling me about a dream he had, featuring his dog and a garden hose that turned into a snake, or the other way around, I'm not listening very good. Then all of a sudden I remember *my* dream, Meredith dancing for me in just her tennis skirt, and I stand there.

Nathaniel plows into me, sending me sprawling.

I lie there in the cool dirt and bits of stone, still holding the flashlight.

'Y'okay, man?'

I hurt my knee but not very badly.

'Fuck ya *stop* for?' he says.

I get up, wanting to call him something, a surferboy dickwad or something, but I'm determined to keep the silence rule.

'I gotta find that flashlight of mine,' he says.

I shine the light on my face so he can see me nodding.

## about that cross

I mentioned I used to be an altar boy. Jesus loved me in my cassock and surplice, in my crewcut and shiny black shoes. And I loved Him right back. We drifted apart in high school, but for a couple of years there I was a happy lad, in good with the most connected person in the universe. He said it Himself: *No one gets to the Father except through Me.*

Meanwhile, here's what the Zen Buddhists say: *If you meet Buddha on the road, kill him.* Don't hold on to anything—Buddha, Jesus, Elvis—let go, let go, let go.

MEDITATION

**in my robe**

It's gray and hangs down to my ankles, with big sleeves like wings, and when I tie up the waist good and tight I feel ready to go out there and grab me some Enlightenment.

I wouldn't mind seeing how I look, if there was a mirror in here. But that's ego, that's Little Self. I'm here for Big Self.

Out in the dining hall people in their robes are sitting in silence on long wooden benches at long wooden tables sipping coffee or tea or else just sitting, waiting to go upstairs. I pour a cup of coffee and find a place to sit with it. One of my concerns when I came here last week: there wouldn't be any coffee, only tea, *herbal* tea, and I would spend the whole month going through caffeine withdrawal. But at a first-day meeting with the head monk Shugen and the three of us newcomers—me, Nathaniel and Razor—Nathaniel asked him about techniques for staying awake during meditation, and Shugen said, 'The coffee here is brewed very strong.'

He wasn't kidding. One sip and *boing*.

Someone upstairs begins loudly whacking a block of wood with a mallet, meaning it's time.

Heading up these beautiful old stone steps along with the others, everyone holding up their robe so they don't trip on it, I'm feeling like part of the sangha—that's Japanese, meaning the community of fellow seekers. Which is what we are, all of us in this together. Anyway, that's the feeling I have this morning heading up the stairs with everyone. A nice warm feeling.

Then Nathaniel ruins it. The guy's a fucking menace. There's this corridor outside the meditation hall with racks for our shoes and socks and he's hopping all around on one foot trying to yank off his boot and ends up hip-checking some woman, almost knocking her down.

'Hey, sorry,' he whispers.

She stands there giving him an extremely dirty look for a Buddhist. I feel like telling her, *Take it easy, lady? Just take it easy.*

The meditation hall—the Zendo it's called—is big and dim with a polished wooden floor and smells like High Mass. People are sitting on black cushions on black mats in long rows facing a center aisle. On a little altar up at the front a golden Buddha meditates away, flanked by flowers, a tiny smile on his face.

I love that little smile.

Entering, I stop and bow towards the altar, palms together in front of my chin, elbows out, then walk very solemnly to my mat and cushion—my zabuton and zafu, that is. Everything here has a Japanese name, even the monks, even though none of them are Japanese. The whole place is meant to be like a typical Zen Buddhist monastery in Kyoto, where the Abbot had his training. Remember what the ad said? *Rigorous and authentic.* So there you go. Personally, I don't see the problem with calling a mat and a cushion a mat and a cushion instead of a zabuton and a zafu, but what do I know?

Not much.

They've got the three of us starting the last row on the left, near the wall. Razor's on my right, sitting with his legs under him, feet on opposite thighs: the classic full lotus. Nathaniel's on my other side is in half lotus: one foot *under* the thigh instead of on it. And I just sit here straddling the cushion, which is a perfectly legitimate way to sit and even has a Japanese name: seiza.

I've still got some pain in my legs but it's bearable now. That first week, though, was murder. I sat here with actual tears running down my face, that's how bad it was. I ended up going to see one of the senior monks, this guy named Genzo. What a clean little room he had. I told him about the pain in my legs, explaining what a 'distraction' it was, so he wouldn't think I was just being a baby. After listening with full Zen attention, he told me to quit trying to run away.

I said, 'Excuse me?'

He told me to accept the pain. 'Embrace it,' he said. '*Be* it. Get to where you're nothing *but* the pain.'

I told him I was pretty close to that point already.

He shook his shaved head. He said, 'No. Right now there's two of you. There's you and there's the pain. Make them one,' he said, bringing his palms together, showing me what he meant by *one*. 'Then who is left to be distracted by it?' He gave me a little smile. 'Do you see?'

I saw, sort of.

But back on my cushion, no matter how hard I tried, there was still me trying to become one with the pain, plus the pain, which made two.

I went back to Genzo and he gave me some Tylenols.

## lemon drops

Someone in the back taps a little bell, *ding*, meaning it's time to quit shifting around, quit sniffling, quit scratching, quit picturing Meredith dancing for *Lance* now, or Mom doing the hula for Jerry (don't ask), and begin focusing on my breath, silently counting *one* breathing in, *two* breathing out, up to ten then starting over, letting thoughts come, letting them go, building up some real silence here, which I notice, then notice myself noticing, and return to the breath.

Going good...going good...

Then Nathaniel starts sucking on a lemon drop.

I've asked him not to. Just last night in the cabin I told him it's not only disrespectful, it's also very distracting to others.

'What others?' he asked.

'Me, for example,' I said.

He told me he was sorry but he *had* to suck on lemon drops because the incense clogged up his nose so he had to breathe through his mouth which got very dry and the lemon drops helped.

'Yeah, well, could you try not sucking quite so fucking loud?'

He said he would try.

I thanked him, sincerely.

Then he said *I* should try something, too.

'Oh?'

'You should try and lighten *up*, man.'

I nodded, letting my anger rise and float away like a bright red balloon, and told him I would try.

He offered me a lemon drop.

I told him no thank you.

'For later.'

26

'That's all right.'

'I'm trying to be nice here, man.'

'Are you?'

He shook the box at me.

I shook my head at him.

'*Take* one.'

'I don't *want* one,' I told him. 'I don't *like* lemon drops, okay? Is that okay?'

With a weary sigh he stepped up and put a hand on my shoulder: 'See, this is what I'm talking about.'

I told him to get his hand off of me.

'Or what, man?' he said politely, his head cocked, keeping his hand there.

Then Razor in his bed with a book shouted out in his funny Indian accent, 'Stop this! You are behaving like small children!'

He was right. We went to our separate beds.

So now, here I sit, on my cushion, my zafu, trying hard not to hear Nathaniel next to me sucking on a lemon drop as loud as ever. The sucking sound occurs approximately every ten seconds.

There's no way I should know that.

## kinhin

After half an hour the little bell finally dings again and we bow, then get to our feet. Someone in the back whacks a pair of wooden clappers and we turn to the right. He whacks them again and we start doing kinhin—walking meditation—up one row of mats and down the other, single file, trying to step along with complete attention to the cool floor under our bare feet, the swing of our legs inside our robes, even the tiny touch of air on our faces. That's the Zen way. Whatever you're doing, *be* there for it, completely.

Quick Zen story: Two monks are bragging to each other about their Masters. The one says, 'My Master can stand by the river and make beautiful brush strokes appear on a scroll someone is holding on the opposite shore.' The other monk agrees that's pretty good but says *his* Master can do something even more amazing: 'When he eats, he eats. When he sleeps, he sleeps.'

So that's the idea.

I've got Razor in front of me and I can tell he's doing it right, totally just-walking, totally Zen, except for possibly a tiny sliver of his mind admiring how totally Zen he's being. Meanwhile behind me Nathaniel, believe it or not, is quietly humming to himself.

And here's what *I* keep doing. Every time I approach the front of the Zendo where the head monk Shugen sits watching us, I put on this deep scowl to show him how focused I am, or anyway how hard I'm *trying* to be focused. I've been doing that since I got here, every kinhin. Each time I get within sight of Shugen I tell myself, *Don't make the face, don't make the face*, and I make the face.

Why? What do I want? A pat on the head? A good *grade*?
So far I think I'd be pulling a C-.
Nathaniel about the same.
Razor's doing A work but he's proud of it so he's flunking.

**original face**

*Show me your original face, the one you had before your parents were born.*

That's what a long-ago Zen master up on a mountain wanted from his disciple: the face under all the faces he wore. According to the story, the Master's request immediately woke up the disciple's mind—and of course there it was, the face the Master had asked for. But I always imagine the Master *now* wanting to see the face of the one who's showing him *that* face.

And so on.

I imagine them still up on that mountain.

## the kyosaku

After kinhin, another half hour of sitting. No sucking sounds from Nathaniel but I keep waiting for them, then catch myself waiting and scold myself for not staying focused on my breath, then scold myself for wasting time and energy scolding myself instead of heading straight back to the breath—then a loud, echoing *crack* from the other side of the Zendo.

It's Ryushin, one of the senior monks, with the kyosaku, this long narrow wooden paddle he walks around with, slowly, up and down the rows. If you want to be hit with it—to help with drowsiness or wandering thoughts—you put your palms together, elbows out, and he stops in front of you. You bow to one another. Then he whacks you—right shoulder, left shoulder—quick and hard. You bow to each other again and he moves on.

The first time I got the kyosaku I didn't even ask for it, or anyway I didn't *know* I was asking. The way it happened, here came someone on my left, moving slowly along the front of our row, and here was Razor on my right putting his palms together, which I figured he was doing to show respect for whoever was coming, so I did the same: Razor's a professor of world religions—he's written books—so I tend to follow his lead, even though he's kind of a dick. Anyway, imagine my surprise when Ryushin stopped in front of me, bowed, and then walloped me with a canoe paddle. *They found me out!* That's what flashed through my mind. *They found me out!* Then whack, he came down on my other shoulder. Then he bowed to me again. I didn't bow back, though. Fuck him. But then he did the same thing to Razor, and I understood: palms together means *hit me please.*

Anyway, right now it's so quiet I can hear the creak of the floor under Ryushin's footsteps as he makes his rounds. We're facing the wall this period, and as he passes behind me I see his shadow, this tall robed figure taking one slow step, then another, holding the kyosaku in front of him like an executioner's blade. As he comes along the front of the row I put my palms together.

He stops in front of me.

We bow to one another.

He raises back the kyosaku.

I hear a bird outside singing so clearly.

## ryushin

It doesn't hurt very much, by the way, getting whacked with the kyosaku. It *sounds* like he's breaking your bones but it only stings a bit, the way Ryushin does it. I sat across from him at dinner the other night and he was telling me you have to hit the person just right or it *could* hurt, a lot, even do some damage. I told him about the first time I got the kyosaku, last week, how I didn't even realize I was asking for it.

He apologized.

I told him it wasn't his fault.

He wondered what I must have thought.

I told him I thought maybe I was being punished.

'For what?'

'For being fraudulent.' I told him about making phony faces for Shugen during kinhin.

He gave a big laugh.

Ordinarily I would have wanted to know what was so fucking funny. But the way he laughed, shaking his head, it was like he was laughing at how goofy we *all* are, himself included.

I liked Ryushin.

We ate.

'Good soup,' he said.

I agreed. It was vegetable barley, and delicious.

I asked him if he liked pizza.

'*Good* pizza, sure,' he said.

I asked him what he thought of Pizza Hut pizza.

He said he liked the deep-dish kind.

I told him I was a shift manager—*former* shift manager—at a Pizza Hut north of Chicago.

'No kidding.' He seemed interested.

Which is something I've noticed about these Zen folks—they take a real interest. It's not politeness, or not *just* politeness. It's like they've got all this *room* inside for others. Managing a Pizza Hut—trust me, that's a pretty dull subject—but you would have thought I was telling Ryushin about my job as an astronaut.

I explained about making sure the crust was done just right, how it's even trickier with the deep dish, and the way the sauce gets laid on, the toppings evenly distributed—placed on, not thrown on. And then I went too far. I always go too far. 'What it basically comes down to,' I said, 'is caring. Know what I mean?'

'Caring,' he said.

'That's really the *main* ingredient.'

He nodded.

I could tell he had a pretty good idea how much I ever cared about those fucking pizzas.

We ate.

I felt disgusted with myself. I felt like telling him to go get his kyosaku.

MORNING SERVICE

## comin' round the mountain

*Sentient beings are numberless, I vow to save them.*
*The dharmas are boundless, I vow to master them.*
*Desires are inexhaustible, I vow to end them…*

I like chanting along with everyone, reminds me of camp. I went to a summer camp when I was ten and at night we used to sit on these giant logs around a campfire, nice Mr. Underhill strumming a guitar, everyone swaying together while we sang:

*She'll be comin' round the mountain when she comes,*
*She'll be comin' round the mountain when she comes…*

I didn't hit it off with any of the other kids there, especially this fatso named Randy I had to share a tent with, but at night sitting around the campfire, swaying and singing along with everyone, Mr. Underhill strumming away, I enjoyed that quite a lot. The thing I liked about it, as we sang and swayed away, I couldn't tell my own voice from any of the others. There was just this one big voice of all of us. That's what it's like this morning, chanting:

*The Buddha way is unattainable, I vow to attain it…*

'*Stop swaying,*' one of the monks hollers, Ryushin I think.

## the hellhounds

I do have friends, by the way, in case you're wondering. I wouldn't want you to think I'm some kind of a loner. I don't have any *close* friends, the kind you get personal with, but for example I play first base on a slow-pitch softball team every summer with a group of guys I get along with pretty good, for the most part. We call ourselves the Hellhounds—it's on our T-shirts. After the game we usually go for some beers, have some laughs. I try and be careful not to drink too much because whenever I do I tend to gush. That's what our shortstop Larry Murphy told me: 'You tend to gush, Bopper.' I tend to start going on about what a great bunch of guys they are and what an honor to play on the same team with such a great bunch of fucking guys and I'm not just saying that, I really fucking mean it, and so on. It's embarrassing for all concerned. And the thing is? They're really *not* such a great bunch of fucking guys. In fact, some of them are genuine assholes.

## oh buddha, oh perfect one

Some more chanting, bell ringing and bowing down to
Buddha—all the way down, forehead on the floor—which
sounds a little cultish, I know, bowing down like that, but the
way the Abbot explained it last night in his talk, it's not like
you're *worshipping* Buddha, it's more like you're bowing to the
*connection* between the two of you. *You're* a Buddha too, is the
idea. So you *could* say you're bowing to yourself, or anyway the
self we're all trying to get *at* here.

Tell you a secret, though. Sometimes I wish we did worship
Buddha, got down and said to him, *Oh Buddha, I am a miserable*
*piece of utterly worthless dog shit, and you are the Perfect One: all-*
*good, all-wise, all-powerful. Oh save me, Buddha, save me from*
*my miserable dog-shit self!*

That would be so much easier.

FORMAL BREAKFAST

## just enough

It's called oryoki, this very formal, ceremonial-type meal where every single little thing you do has to be absolutely correct. It's supposed to help you be mindful, be here and now, be Zen. At yesterday's breakfast downstairs in the dining hall they had a run-through for us newcomers.

What a disaster that was.

Someone who'd been here a while was sitting across the table for me to try and follow, but I was so nervous my brain seized up. So, for example, when he placed his little spatula at the bottom left-hand corner of his little table cloth, facing out, and laid his chopsticks above the spatula, facing in, I couldn't work out his left and mine, above versus below, in versus out. Meanwhile I had this monk named Hitoshi sitting next to me whispering in my ear, 'Something is wrong with your bowls and utensils. Can you see what it is?'

I looked over at Nathaniel hoping to see him struggling worse than me, but he seemed to be doing fine, as of course was Razor.

'Pay attention,' Hitoshi whispered. 'Place your mind entirely on your bowls and utensils. They are not aligned properly.'

I came *this close* to walking out and driving home where I could align my bowls and utensils any goddam way I pleased.

Then, finally, came the actual Eating of the Meal. Which I figured we were supposed to do very slowly and deliberately, putting extra attention on the tastes and textures of the food. So that's what I was trying to do, eyes lowered, chewing ponderously, like a cow. But after a little while I noticed Hitoshi next to me was already done, sitting there with his hands in his lap. Then I noticed *everyone* was sitting there with their hands in their lap, waiting for me to finish. And I still had all my cantaloupe chunks to go. I like cantaloupe and had taken quite a lot. So now I began stabbing the chunks with one of my chopsticks, mouthing them and chewing like mad. Then I started swallowing them almost whole. The very last one got stuck in my throat—*Oh God, not like this*—and I stood straight up, throwing my arms out wide as if blessing everyone, and managed to swallow, and sat back down.

'Are you all right?' Hitoshi whispered.

I nodded.

'You sure?'

I nodded.

Some chanting after that. Then afterwards the Washing of the Bowls, which I got through all right—there wasn't that much you could screw up. But then we had to tie up our kits—our bowls and utensils—using our individual little table cloth/napkin.

'Make a lotus flower,' Hitoshi whispered.

'Sorry?'

'Make one tail of your knot resemble a lotus flower.'

Was he serious?

He nodded towards the guy across from me, who had one tail of his knot standing up straight and was carefully spreading out the sides—it looked more like a cobra snake. Then he put his hands in his lap.

So once again everyone was waiting for me, Hitoshi finally whispering, 'Just leave it.'

Then a closing chant about accomplishing our Buddha Way.

Afterwards Hitoshi asked me to stay behind.

We sat there waiting for the others to leave. I wanted to tell him Nathaniel sucks on lemon drops in the Zendo and talks during quiet hours and leaves his clothes all over the cabin floor.

'Do you know what the word 'oryoki' means?' Hitoshi asked.

I tried to think. 'Something like…'ceremonial meal'?'

'It means 'Just enough'.'

My face went hot. 'The cantaloupe. You're right. I took way too much.'

He shook his bald head. 'That's not what I'm saying. 'Just enough' means...' He paused. 'Tell you what,' he said, 'why don't you think about what it means.'

'Right now? Think about it right now?'

'While you're here with us. You're here for the month, right?'

'Right.' *Another three weeks*, I thought. *Jesus*, I thought.

'Have it there in your mind,' he said. 'What is 'Just enough?' Let it work.'

'Like a koan, you mean?'

He smiled. 'If you like.'

A koan is a question a Zen teacher gives a student to try and work on. It's not something you can figure out an answer to and in fact they don't even usually make any sense, like the most famous one: *What is the sound of one hand clapping?* Try figuring *that* out. You can't. The answer has to come from a place way deeper than thinking goes. Anyway, I liked having my own koan: *What is the meaning of 'Just enough'?*

Hitoshi took me through the entire oryoki ceremony again, moment by moment, with imaginary food, being very patient. I felt sick to my stomach with embarrassment, gratitude, and cantaloupe chunks.


So that was yesterday, the rehearsal. This morning we're doing the real oryoki, right here in the Zendo, kneeling on our mats, and I'm on my own. But it goes pretty well, in fact *very* well. Thanks to Hitoshi's help yesterday, I feel confident enough about my bowls and utensils to relax, and relaxed enough to put heart and soul into each little bit of oryoki business, setting this bowl exactly next to that one, spatula precisely over here, chopsticks lined up thusly.

The servers come around offering oatmeal, apple slices and

orange juice. To be on the safe side, I show with my thumb and finger: *small portions please.*

There's some chanting:

*As we desire the natural order of mind,*

*To be free from clinging, we must be free from greed,*

and so on.

Then we start eating. And oh my God, the oatmeal—it's so oatmealy! And the apple slices—such appleness! I've never tasted food so clearly. And it's because, you see, I've been so mindful with my bowls and utensils, which has carried over into mindfully eating:

*When you eat, just eat.*

So now I kind of wish I took a little more.

But see, that's greed, that's clinging to the experience instead of letting it happen and pass. On the other hand, taking too *little* can be greedy too: greedy about being non-greedy.

I think I might be closing in on my koan here, on the meaning of 'Just enough': something about, first of all, on the one hand…

Ah fuck it, just eat.

I finish with the others.

And then at the end, tying up our kits, making a lotus flower, I finish well ahead of Nathaniel on my left and even a little ahead of Razor on my right.

I'm not bragging, I'm just saying.

-

## adrift

So that was an excellent oryoki, especially the oatmeal and apple slices. Ordinarily I hardly notice what I'm eating. If it's salty enough I could be eating fried rice or fried lice, that's how much attention I pay. And not just to eating, either. Lately I've begun noticing the amount of time I spend somewhere else, adrift in daydreams.

It's amazing.

And depressing.

If I was on my deathbed right now, I would have plenty of regrets, but by far the biggest one would have to be: *For most of the moments of my life, I wasn't there.*

BODY PRACTICE

## dear bopper, dear mom

After breakfast I check my mail slot in the hallway off the Zendo. There's a letter! It's only from my mom, but still.

*Dear Bopper,*

*How are you, hon? I hope it's working out for you there. But if it's not, don't feel like you have to stay. You'll always have a place back here, I hope you know that, until you can find something.*

*I was looking through some of the books in those boxes you left and I have to say I don't exactly understand what Zen Buddhism is supposed to do for you, although I'm sure you know what you're doing so I'm not going to worry, although I can't help wondering what's wrong with good old Jesus if you're feeling the need for religion.*

*Jerry's putting in a red brick patio in the backyard. We're going to get one of those umbrella tables. It's going to be nice. We can sit out there and drink lemonade and play gin—or the other way around, ha-ha.*

*He said to say hello, by the way.*

*I know the two of you haven't gotten along very well and I certainly don't expect you to think of Jerry as some kind of father or anything like that, but I can't help feeling if the two of you got to know each other better you could be friends, or maybe not friends but at least be friendly, or anyway civil.*

*Work is going good lately. I sold a house yesterday! People are finally starting to borrow money again. Jerry says it's because of our new president's sunny patriotic attitude. Jimmy Carter was a nice enough man, but like they say in the beer commercial, 'Who says you can't have it all?'*

*We're going out to dinner tonight to celebrate my sale, probably to*

*Cavallini's. By the way, how's the food there? Not too odd I hope, seaweed and such.*

*Let me hear from you, Bopper. You know me, I worry. You quit your job and drive off to the Catskill Mountains to join a religious cult—how am I not supposed to worry? So let me know you're doing okay, which I'm sure you are, but let me know anyway. Thanks, hon.*

*Jerry says dress warm.*
*Love always,*
*Mom*


*Hi Mom,*

*Just got your letter. Thanks. That patio sounds like it's going to be nice. Congratulations on selling a house, that's really great.*

*It's going okay here. The food is pretty good, not too weird, no meat but that's all right, although if you handed me a cheeseburger right now I wouldn't say no thank you! Have you ever heard of tofu? It's supposed to be good for you. It's Japanese. Practically everything here is Japanese, where Zen comes from. The last two mornings we had to use chopsticks, no choice. Boy, those sure are tricky!*

*I know you probably think this whole thing is pretty weird, sometimes I do too, but I'm going to try and stick it out. For one thing, you don't get a refund if you quit early. Also, remember that laughing Buddha cookie jar we had? You used to say you couldn't look at it without smiling just a little, no matter what kind of mood you were in.*

*At night I'm sleeping in an actual log cabin. It's not bad, no heat but plenty of heavy blankets. These two guys I'm in there with are okay. One is a little older than me, from India, a professor over there, kind of stuck on himself. The other one's a little younger than me, from southern California, with a long pony tail. He gets on my nerves a little, sometimes a lot.*

*Anyway, I'm doing fine. So don't worry, okay?*

*Well, I have to go now. Yoga next. Want a good laugh? Picture*

*me doing yoga!*
*Bye, Mom.*
*Love, Bopper*

## dad

*Jerry says dress warm.*

I'm sure.

Mom doesn't push it but I know she would like it a lot if I started thinking of Jerry as my dad. But there's no way. For one thing, I already have a father. I don't remember him, he died when I was three, but that's not *his* fault. Or actually, it sort of was. He got killed trying to run a red light. The other driver was okay. According to Mom, Dad was driving home from the bar. She says he drank a lot. I guess I believe her but I have to say he looks totally sober throughout this entire giant photo album she has: tall and bony and sharp-eyed. In one of the pictures he's holding me as a baby, a big proud grin on his face, displaying me like a fish he caught. I look completely bewildered. I haven't changed much.

Dad, by the way, is the one who gave me the name Bopper. My actual name is Carl, after my dad's dad. But according to Mom, when I was learning to walk, Dad liked the way I went stomping around, nodding my head—*bopping* around—so he called me Bopper, and it stuck.

Dad was a lineman for Bell Telephone, like in that old Glen Campbell song, *Wichita Lineman*.

As a kid I used to imagine him still up there at the top of a pole, in his hard hat and tool belt, looking down on me, seeing me wherever I was. Practically everything I did made him proud, even something like tying my shoes:

—*You tied those real nice and tight, Bopper. I'm proud of you.*

—*Thanks, Dad.*

As I got older, though, he started criticizing my behavior:

—*Leave your dick alone, son.*

*—Sorry, Dad.*

Eventually I went ahead and let him be dead.

One thing I've always wondered, though. At the very last moment, did he see the other car coming? Was there a moment, just one split second, when he thought *Oh fuck*?

Just that.

*Oh fuck.*

**slugs, anchovies**

We have to make room in the dining hall for yoga, and as everyone energetically begins moving tables and benches against the wall I stand there admiring their wholeheartedness. Then someone grabs one end of a nearby table and looks at me, and I grab the other end.

After the hall is cleared we sit on the floor anywhere we want. I sit all the way in the very back behind everyone: I'm terrible at this yoga stuff—way too long and stiff—and don't wish to be seen.

Everyone gets to their feet as this energetic little bald-headed female monk named Jinmon enters wearing a body stocking and a blinding smile. She bows, we bow. Instructors are allowed to speak during silence period, and with this cheerful, irritating voice she leads us for the next hour through a bunch of different postures. Ordinarily I try but today I'm taking it easy back here. Remember earlier, coming down the hill, when Nathaniel knocked me over? Well, my knee still hurts a little, if I concentrate hard enough. Mostly though, to be honest, I just don't feel like doing this shit today.

'Now hold that position,' Jinmon is telling them. 'Place all of your attention on the breath. That's it, stay with the breath... stay with it...staaay...'

You can tell Razor's done a lot of this before. I'll bet he could probably even pretzel himself into some of those shocking postures you see really advanced yoga guys get into. I can picture him in a Gandhi diaper with his feet locked behind his neck, standing on his head over a bed of nails, that same smug look on his smooth brown face, only upside down.

Meanwhile, on the other side of the room, Nathaniel is doing his laidback best.

Then something very embarrassing happens. Jinmon has everyone get into a posture that involves turning their hips and looking behind them. So all of a sudden here's all these people looking over their shoulder at me sitting back here taking it easy. My first impulse is to start rubbing my knee with a scowl to show how unhappy I am that I can't join in. But I surprise myself and don't do that. I don't do anything. I just sit here letting them go ahead and look at me if they want. I don't even lower my eyes.

'Stay with it,' Jinmon is saying, 'staaay with it.'

I stay with it.


The hour ends with her turning out the lights and telling us to lie on our backs, eyes closed, arms along our sides. This one I'm willing to do. She speaks to us quietly now: 'Just let go... just let go...'

I'm trying to. But the problem is, what am I trying to let go of? Myself. And who's trying to do the letting go? I am. See the problem?

Even so, I'm tired enough that I end up falling asleep. I dream I'm at work, at the Pizza Hut. A customer calls me over. He's outraged, pointing at his pizza. *Those aren't anchovies*, he says, *those are slugs*. I touch his shoulder and tell him gently, *Slugs, anchovies...what's the difference?* His face lights up with understanding. I pat his shoulder: *Enjoy your pizza.*

The overhead lights go on and off, on and off: nap time over. We get up and start moving the tables and benches back. I throw myself into it, feeling refreshed.

WORK PRACTICE

**squirrel**

Another break before we have to meet back in the dining hall for work assignments, forty-five minutes to do anything we want except speak—which is no hardship: I've got nothing to say to anyone. What's *not* so easy: staying quiet *inside*.

Right now for instance I'm yakking away in my head while I march up the hill to the bathhouse where I'm hoping to do something about this block of cement my bowels are turning into. There's plenty of toilets in the main building, real ones that flush, but I can't relax there, people coming in and out, so I'm silently talking to myself now about being back in my apartment, how nice it would be with my own bathroom, a good Zen book and all the time in the world. But then I remember: I don't have an apartment anymore. I'll be with Mom—and Jerry—until I find something. Which is okay. I can take it for a while. I just wish he wouldn't boss her around so much, calling her 'Babe,' as in, *Grab me a beer while you're up, will ya, Babe?* And you know what she calls *him* sometimes? 'Big Daddy.' *Sure thing, Big Daddy,* she'll say, and then this fucking *smile* comes over his fat oily face. Makes me want to skull him with one of his bottles of Hawaiian beer. Jesus, every fucking thing is Hawaiian with that guy. He went to Honolulu once on a sales trip and he must have had one hell of a good time because now he only drinks Aloha Lager, wears the ugly flowered shirts, watches reruns of *Hawaii Five-0*, listens to entire *albums* of hula music, and here's something I wish I could somehow erase from my brain: One Sunday afternoon I made the mistake of dropping by without calling first. A hula album—ukulele and slide guitar—was turned up loud. I found them out in the kitchen, Mom hula dancing in a fake grass skirt with a pink paper lei over her droopy naked boobs, while he sat there in his underwear watching her, like some fat Hawaiian king, the table full of empty Aloha bottles. And here's the worst part. Instead of grabbing one of the empties and beating him over the head with it, I carefully tiptoed backwards out of there.

A squirrel comes racing noisily through the dry leaves, leaps onto a tree, scurries halfway up, then stops dead still and stares at me. I stand there, dead still, staring back. Maybe five entire seconds pass. *I am one with this squirrel*, I think to myself, which breaks the spell and he scampers up the tree.

I continue up the path.

Anyway, that's an image I would do anything to get rid of, Mom hula dancing half-naked for drunken Jerry in his underwear. I would run a red hot poker straight through my brain if I thought it would help.

### genuine zen monk

My visit to the john turns out to be a tremendous success, and I hurry back down the hill as light as a butterfly. Somewhere in my Buddha books there's a tale about a Chinese guy who dreamed one night he was a butterfly and afterwards was never sure if he was a man who dreamed he was a butterfly or a butterfly dreaming he was a man. I like that story, especially how he seemed okay with it either way.

When I get to the dining hall everyone is standing there reciting a chant I still haven't memorized, and I hum along. Afterwards Jinmon begins reading out our work assignments for this morning.

When I first came here I was hoping to get either bathrooms or leaves. I figured cleaning bathrooms would be good for my ego, meaning bad for it, which is good, ego being the main thing that stands between you and enlightenment. And raking leaves, well, that's what I always picture Zen monks doing, like in those little anecdotes where one of them says to the other, *Does a squirrel have Buddha nature?* And the other one answers, *I am using this rake with full awareness.*

But they gave me vacuuming.

I had to go around vacuuming every carpet in the main building. I couldn't make any Zen connection to vacuuming and had all kinds of trouble with the extension cord and wanted to go home. But I stayed. And the next day they gave me vacuuming again. But this time I didn't worry about the Zen of vacuuming, and it went a lot better. Whether I was using the vacuum with full awareness or not, the carpets were looking good.

They gave me vacuuming all week. I was actually getting

quite skillful at it. I was even beginning to think of myself as the Master of Vacuuming. But they never let you do that here, let you get comfortable, get *settled*. They're always pulling the rug out, or the carpet.

So today they assign me leaf raking.

They've put me and Razor and Nathaniel together. One of the monks—Genzo, the guy who gave me the Tylenol for my legs—takes us to the shed where he hands out rakes and tells us to do the area between the main building and the vegetable garden. He points to a large, rolled-up tarp on the floor against the wall: 'Take it out, unroll it, and rake as many leaves onto it as possible, then carry it over to the creek, but don't dump the leaves in the water, rake them along the embankment, spreading them out evenly, then return with the tarp, lay it in the space you've already raked, and repeat.' He says all this in a smooth quiet voice, arms along his sides, looking sincerely at each of us in turn. Then he bows, palms together, and walks off.

I thought maybe he'd ask me how my legs are doing.

We carry the tarp out and unroll it on the grass. It's a nice day for November, pretty mild, especially when the sun comes out, which it keeps doing, then slipping under again. We begin raking. No one speaks, about an hour more of silence to go.

So: here I am, raking leaves, like a genuine Zen monk. Except, of course, a genuine Zen monk wouldn't be thinking to himself, *Here I am raking leaves like a genuine Zen monk*. He would just be raking leaves.

So: Here I am, just raking leaves, like a genuine Zen monk.

## genuine u.s. marshal

When I was little I enjoyed pretending I was a U.S. marshal. I had a gun and holster, a cowboy hat, and a tin star pinned to my T-shirt. I had to kill a lot of people. I even shot my Dennis the Menace doll, right in his smart-aleck face. I was sorry but I had no choice: I had to keep order. Then someone who looked like me rode into town telling everyone *he* was the marshal, this left-handed imposter in the mirror over the dresser. So we had a showdown. I was fast but he was just as fast and we shot each other. I remember standing there, still holding out my gun, looking at him holding out his. I felt bad for him, and I could see he felt bad for me, too. Then we both dropped our gun and fell to the carpet. I laid there for a long time, I remember, wondering what to do with myself next.

## an astounding thing

Razor is wearing a watch and announces it's ten o'clock and we can talk now. 'If we wish to,' he adds.

We all continue silently raking for a while.

Nathaniel finally breaks the ice: 'I'm horny.'

Razor tells him he should use that to bring greater strength to his meditation.

Nathaniel says he'd rather use it to have sex.

'I'm afraid I cannot help you there.'

'I wasn't *asking* you to.'

Razor then begins explaining about meditation and the various energy centers, using a lot of Hindu-sounding terms.

Nathaniel interrupts him. 'So you're saying, what, I'm not gonna want sex at *all* after enlightenment? That what you're saying?'

Razor gives this little giggle of his. 'I don't think that's a question you need to overly concern yourself with.'

Nathaniel's big blue eyes get even bigger. 'Fuck's *that* suppose to mean?'

I interrupt, 'I think this thing is full enough now,' meaning the tarp.

They agree, and at the count of three we lift it and walk with it towards the little creek. There's a lot of shrubbery and large rocks on the way so it's tricky and we're all shouting instructions. By the time we reach the embankment, half the load is gone. We dump what's left. Then Razor says we need to spread the leaves out evenly, as we were instructed, and tells me to go get the rakes.

Nathaniel wants to know who died and left *him* boss. I'm wondering too.

Razor doesn't understand the question: 'Who *died*?'

Nathaniel is explaining while I go get the rakes.

Then, while heading back, I have an Experience. The whole thing lasts maybe five seconds. I'm walking along with the three rakes over my shoulder, the sun behind some clouds again, a little breeze on my face, and that's it, nothing is different, except all of a sudden it's happening right now, this very moment, and I'm here for it, completely. I'm walking along completely here!

Something from the Abbot's talk the other night occurs to me: *What an astounding thing it is, to exist.*

So this is what he meant.

Only, now I'm not so completely here anymore: I'm *thinking* about being completely here, which isn't the same. By the time I'm handing out the rakes the whole thing has fled, like that squirrel earlier.

Nathaniel says this isn't the rake he was using.

I tell him tough shit.

**chiyono's bucket**

I know what I did wrong. I tried to turn the moment into something I could hold onto, something I could *have*.

Like Chiyono.

She was this long-ago Buddhist nun who had a brief little awakening experience and afterwards was doing what I was: trying to hold on to it. The Abbot told us about her the other night, in that same dharma talk. He said one night Chiyono was returning from the well with an old patched-up wooden bucket full of water, with the beautiful white moon reflected in it. She was stepping along carefully, not wanting to lose the water, not wanting to lose the beautiful white moon. Then suddenly the bottom of the bucket fell out—*woosh*, there goes the water, there goes the moon.

'At that moment,' the Abbot said, 'Chiyono had her Full Awakening.'

I have this clear picture of her standing there in her kimono, in the moonlight, holding the empty bucket, laughing quietly.

## fifth graders

After we drag the tarp back and start covering it with leaves again I ask if either of them know what the word 'oryoki' means. I figure maybe they can give me a little help with my koan. The truth is, I'm starting to get impatient. I was given a little five-second glimpse of what it's like to be completely present, completely alive, then the door was slammed in my face, or I guess *I* slammed it, but anyway I'm beginning to get impatient with this whole fucking quest.

Razor says 'oryoki' is a Japanese word meaning 'ceremonial meal.'

'*Wrong*,' I pounce. 'It *is* Japanese and it *is* a ceremonial meal, but it means 'Just enough'.'

'Just enough what?' says Nathaniel.

'That's what I'm wondering. I got this from Hitoshi. He gave it to me after breakfast yesterday: *What is the meaning of 'Just enough'?* He told me to work on it.'

'As a koan?' Razor asks.

'You could say.'

I can tell he's wondering how come *he* didn't get a koan.

Koan envy.

'I'd say the meaning's pretty basic,' Nathaniel tells me. 'Means just what it says.'

'Which is?'

He gives a little grin: "Don't be a pig'.'

Razor giggles.

So now I'm pissed off. 'Are you talking about the cantaloupe yesterday? Because if you are, first of all I was eating too *slow*, okay? That was the problem.'

'I don't know,' Nathaniel drawls. 'Looked to me like an awful lot of—'

'*Second* of all, a koan has to be a lot deeper than 'Don't be a pig'.'
'As it happens,' says Razor in this calm professor's voice, meaning he is now going to settle the matter, 'you are both in a sense correct. 'Just enough' indicates the Middle Way. And that is extremely simple and at the same time extremely 'deep', as you say.' He goes on for a while then about the Buddhist doctrine of the Middle Way.

And I'm sure he's probably right. I mean I'm sure that's probably the correct answer to the question, *What is the meaning of 'Just enough'*? Except, that's not what I'm looking for, correct versus incorrect. But that's probably the only kind of answer I'm likely to get, going outside for it.

When Razor finally finishes his lecture on the Middle Way, Nathaniel asks him, 'What's the sound of one hand clapping? Answer *that* one.'

'Don't be foolish,' Razor tells him.

'*That's* what it means? 'Don't be foolish'?'

'No, I am telling *you*: Don't be foolish.'

Nathaniel goes into his quiet, puzzled routine: 'Why you calling me foolish, man?'

Razor tells him, 'Because you would never understand the answer, because you would first need to understand the question, which you clearly do not, or you would never ask for the answer!'

Nathaniel steps calmly over and puts a hand on Razor's shoulder: 'You need to lighten up, my friend.'

Razor tells him, 'Please remove yourself or I will demonstrate the sound of one hand *slapping*.'

Nathaniel cocks his head: 'Are you threatening me, man?'

'*For fuck sake*,' I shout.

They look at me.

'What're you, a pair of *fifth* graders?'

Nathaniel tells me where to shove my rake. Before I can come back with something, Razor hotly informs me he is *not* in the fifth grade, that he's a professor of comparative religion who's written three books and he would like to know if *I've* written three books or even *one*.

'Maybe not,' I tell him. 'But I have a koan. Do *you* have a koan? Either *one* of you fuckers?'

Nathaniel says he doubts if that's even a koan. 'How'd it go again?'

I tell him carefully, 'What...is the meaning...of 'Just...enough'?'

'So how's that a koan? You can't just call *any* question a fucking koan.'

Razor says to me, 'I am afraid our young friend here is correct.'

I give a laugh. 'You're agreeing with Nathaniel? Now I *know* you're desperate.'

'Hey, fuck you,' Nathaniel tells me.

'Yeah? Fuck *you*,' I tell him. 'And you,' I tell Razor while I'm at it.

'And you as well,' Razor tells me.

So, we got *that* settled anyway. We go back to raking.

**spat**

I remember a little exchange I had with Meredith. It was after she started her tennis lessons with Zen master Lance. She kept on quoting him:

'Lance says you make your own luck.'

'Lance says the net is your best friend.'

'Lance says winning is just losing spelled backwards.'

'No it's not,' I said.

'Not what?'

'Losing isn't winning spelled backwards.'

'No, he said *winning* is *losing* spelled backwards.'

'It should work either way.'

'He didn't mean it literally, Bopper. You always take things literally. Lance says people who always—'

*'Aw, fuck Lance, will ya?'*

I didn't mean it literally.

LUNCH

**arthur**

I'm in line behind a cheerful little gray-bearded guy named Arthur. I don't think he knows *my* name but he's always very friendly to me, to everyone in fact.

'*So,*' he says, 'how are *you* today?'

I wonder if he was always like this, or did Zen have something to do with it. I like to think he used to be someone like me but started doing Zen, then rose from his cushion one day with the warm friendly smile he's wearing now.

I tell him I'm doing okay.

He touches my arm. 'Good,' he says. 'I'm glad.' And he really seems to mean it, nodding and smiling up into my face.

So I nod and smile down into his, what the hell, and ask him, 'How about *you*? How are *you* doing today?'

'Me? Oh, I'm doing fine,' he says, 'just fine.'

I tell him I'm very glad to hear it.

But I'm not, I realize. Not really. The truth is, I don't give a shit how he's doing. I don't even know the fucking guy.

'This looks wonderful,' he says as we reach the food table.

'Uh-huh.'

I'm glad he doesn't wait for me but goes ahead and sits somewhere.

**radishes**

I find a place at a table next to this middle-aged woman named Sarah, who I've heard is an ex-nun. Before sitting down I set my tray on the table, place my palms together, and bow to the stir-fried vegetables and tofu I am about to eat. The Abbot says everything we do, no matter how small and unimportant we think it is, should be equally sacred, an equally sacred act. But I don't really know what that word actually means, 'sacred'. I wonder if Sarah the ex-nun would possibly have some thoughts. Maybe that's why she left the nunnery, you know? If everything is sacred, why bother being a nun?—or for that matter, a Zen Buddhist. I'd like to have a chat with her sometime.

Right now though, she's talking across the table to this baldheaded old-lady monk named Hojin who runs the giant vegetable garden they've got here. They're talking about radishes, how to plant them properly and nurture them. I've never liked radishes. I don't know how anyone could. Hot little horrible things.

'I hate radishes.'

They look at me.

'Sorry, it slipped out.'

'I don't know your name,' Sarah says, in a nice way.

'It's Bopper.'

'Mine is Sarah.'

'Right. Hi.'

'Have you met Hojin?'

'Hello, Bopper.'

'You run the garden, right?'

'That's right. Do you like to garden, Bopper?'

'Never tried.' I turn back to Sarah: 'Can I ask you something?

I know you're an ex-nun—I'm an ex-altar boy myself—so I was wondering, if it's not too personal: What made you quit?'

'Oh dear,' she says, and gives a big sigh, like that is *such* a long story.

I tell her my theory: 'If everything is sacred, why be a nun, right? Might as well be a sacred mailman, or a sacred *real* estate agent, like my mom, although she's not sacred—or maybe she is, I don't know. That's my point: What does that word really mean?'

"Sacred'?'

'Do you know?'

She draws a long breath. 'Well...*I suppose* I would say...'

But Hojin jumps in with *her* notion, which is: when something she's planted starts poking up through the ground. 'Striving towards the light,' she says. 'That's as sacred as anything *I* know.'

Sarah smiles at her. 'Hojin, that is so beautiful.'

I agree. Only, I'm not looking for beautiful, I'm looking for some kind of *definition* here. But I guess it's like with my koan, you can't go outside for it. So I thank them with a nod and a smile, like *now* I've got it, and return to my vegetables and tofu. They return to their discussion of radishes.

Just for a moment I feel so lonely I could let my face fall into my plate.

## speaking of radishes

The man pulling radishes
pointed my way
with a radish.

– Issa

**rachel**

I'm on lunchtime cleanup crew, probably for the week. Yesterday I was bussing tables. Today I'm washing dishes. It's stupid to think of it as a promotion, but I do.

I've got two big stainless steel sinks in front of me, one with hot water and thick suds, the other one empty for rinsing. Next to me there's a skinny, pissed-off-looking woman about my age named Rachel waiting with a dish towel to dry and put away what I hand her.

I'm trying very hard to wash each pot and pan, each plate, each bowl and utensil, with full Zen awareness, focusing for example on this particular serving bowl and the washing of it, appreciating its bowlness, which I stroke with the sudsy sponge. Then I turn all of my attention to the rinsing of it, the suds sliding off under the jet of hot water, fingers of steam caressing my face...

'Know what?' says Rachel in her sharp voice. 'It might go better if we trade places,' handing me the dish towel.

I have to work like mad to keep up with the pots and pans and fistfuls of silverware she keeps dumping in front of me, and I know damn well she's working doubly fast to make me feel doubly foolish for the stupid, moony way *I* was doing them.

I hate her.

Not really.

Yes I do, really.

But then, when we're finished, she stands there in front of me, presses her palms together, elbows out, and bends down low.

So I do the same.

And just like that, we're okay, completely. We still don't *like* each other very much, but that's beside the point.

So I'm thinking maybe I have it backwards, you know? About the meaning of 'sacred'. Maybe you don't first learn the meaning, then go around bowing to things. Maybe it's by bowing to things you learn the meaning.

Or begin to get an inkling.

**eating jesus**

Growing up, the most sacred thing I knew was, of course, that little white wafer. It wasn't a symbol. He didn't say, *Try and think of this bread as my body.* He said, *This is my body. Eat it. It's good for you.*

But don't chew, we were told. Don't be biting Our Lord. Let Him dissolve on your tongue and slide on down to your soul. Then you'll have Him inside. Then your soul will be a tabernacle, like the one on the altar, that little golden house. And if you keep it clean, when you die He'll take you up to that *big* golden house. But let it get dirty and you'll be thrown into Hell where you'll scream and scream and no one will hear, not even Jesus.

*Corpus Domini nostri.* That's what Father mumbled, laying a wafer on everyone's trembling tongue, while I held the paten under their chin to catch any crumbs. *Corpus Domini nostri*: the body of Our Lord.

The wafers came in boxes of a hundred, ten rows of ten little bodies of Our Lord in a cardboard box with a handy lid.

ART PRACTICE

**what the brush wants**

'The brush knows where to go,' Teacher tells us, walking around.

We're a small group—me, Razor, Nathaniel and two women—each of us kneeling on the library floor over a large sheet of drawing paper, with a paint brush and a shallow bowl of ink.

'Allow the brush to go where it will.'

Teacher's a skinny little guy in a black robe and sandals, Japanese or Chinese, anyway Asian, with long gray hair and a long gray beard, bad teeth, and alert little eyes. He's a visiting artist, just arrived, and wants us to call him simply 'Teacher'.

'Stay out of the brush's way,' he tells us.

You put some ink on the tip of your brush, take a long deep breath, and as you slowly let it out you touch the brush to the paper and see where it leads you, like with a Ouija board. My brush leads me in a big wide circle, nice and round. The brush seems satisfied with that but I go ahead and add two little dabs for the eyes, a stroke for the nose, and a big curving line for a happy Buddha smile.

'Did your brush wish for you to make a smiley face?' Teacher wants to know, standing over me.

I sit back on my heels. 'Not really,' I tell him. 'I just felt like it needed more.'

'More than what?'

'Than just a circle.'

'I see,' he says. 'So you are telling the brush what to do?'

'I thought I'd give it a little help.'

'The brush does not need your help,' he says. 'Do you think you know more than the brush?'

I look up at him. 'To be honest? Yeah, I think I do.'

He smiles, sad and wise. 'So. This is something you must work on.' He bows and moves along.

I add a pair of ears and some nice eyebrows.

Teacher stands over Razor nodding down at what *he's* done. It looks like some kind of Japanese lettering.

'The character for enlightenment,' Teacher says.

Razor nods, looking pleased with himself.

'I am puzzled,' Teacher says. 'May I ask? How does your brush, a mere brush, know the Japanese character for enlightenment?'

Razor doesn't say.

'You must remain out of the way,' Teacher tells him. 'You must learn to stay out of the way completely,' he says, then bows and moves on.

Razor sits there staring straight ahead, taking long, steady breaths.

Teacher has some mild compliments for the two women, but says they're still 'holding the leash.' He says we have to let go of the leash, let the dog run wherever it wishes.

The last drawing he comes to is Nathaniel's. 'Yes,' he says, nodding down at it. I can see from here it's just a bunch of careless-looking swipes. 'Yes,' Teacher says again.

'See, I *have* a dog,' Nathaniel explains, 'a chocolate lab, and I never use a leash.'

'Your dog is free.'

'Totally, man.'

'You have understood.'

'Want me to hold it up? Show the others?'

'Not necessary.'

After class Nathaniel wants me and Razor to know he thought *our* paintings were good, too. 'Seriously. I'm not just saying that.'

## juggling

I don't like Teacher very much but he's right, what he says about staying out of the way. For instance, I remember in high school wanting to be a juggler. I saw this guy on TV juggling bowling pins and telling jokes all the while, which seemed like a very cool thing to be able to do. I wanted to be popular and that seemed like a good way to get there. I pictured an assembly in the gym, our principal Mr. Renfrow saying into the microphone, 'And now, to bring us a little entertainment, here's Bopper!' And I would come walking out, already juggling.

I practiced in my room with three small apples, over my bed so when I dropped them they were right there. I figured out a way of doing the three. It's not that hard. Except, you have to keep not thinking about it. As soon as you do, as soon as you think about how you're doing it—tossing, in an arc, one of the two apples you're holding in your left hand, then tossing the one apple you're holding in your right hand, then catching the first apple with your now-empty right hand, meanwhile tossing the remaining apple in your left hand in time to catch the one coming down from your right hand—as soon as you start thinking about all that while you're doing it, down they all come.

But if you're *trying* not to think about it, telling yourself *don't think about it*, that's just as bad. Down they come.

As Teacher says, 'You must remain completely out of the way.'

I tried telling a joke while I juggled, trying to stay focused on the joke and not notice what my hands were doing:

'Monkey walks into a bar, sits on a stool, says to the bartender...'

Shit.

'Monkey walks into a bar, sits on a stool...'
Shit.
'Monkey walks into a bar...'
*Shit.*
After a while I finally gave up. I sat down on the bed. I decided juggling probably wouldn't make me popular anyway. You had to be either good looking or, if not, have a really good personality. I ate the apples, one after the other, all three, with big violent bites.

**the abbot**

After art class I'm in an out-of-the-way bathroom I've discovered upstairs from the library, standing there just beginning to pee. Then someone walks in and takes the other urinal. I try and see from the corner of my eye if it's anyone I recognize.

Oh my God it's the Abbot.

He's in overalls and a red flannel shirt instead of his robes but it's him all right—great big baldheaded guy, it's him. The connection between my bladder and my penis closes up completely.

I've only met him once, in what's called a dokusan. You go into this room where he's sitting on a little platform, walk up, kneel down and tell him about some problem you're having in your practice. I went in and told him everything was fine: A-okay. He lifted his Zen Master eyes and looked at me. I told him things could be better, of course. He continued looking at me. I told him I was lost and confused and extremely constipated. He told me to avoid dairy products. Then he rang his little handbell, meaning our visit was over.

And now, here we are, side by side with our wangers out. Except, he's actually using his—I can hear the hiss and trickle. After a minute he gives a little bounce, zips up, hits the flusher, and steps serenely over to the sink. He runs water over his hands, turning them. He then gives his complete attention to wiping them with a paper towel. After that, he crumples up the paper towel, drops it in the garbage, and leaves.

I resume peeing.

WORK PRACTICE

**an actual horse**

I check the schedule on the bulletin board in the dining hall:
3:00, Work Practice.

Christ.

I'm tired of working here. I know it's part of the training and
I know the Zen saying, 'Isn't it marvelous? I chop wood and
carry water.' But it *isn't* marvelous. It's long and boring and we
don't get paid. I hate working for nothing. There, I've said it.

Right now it's only two-fifteen: forty-five minutes to do
whatever. I try to think of something. It might be nice to go up
to the cabin and flop on the bed and read for a while, or even
just lie there staring up at the ceiling. But walking there and
back you're losing twenty minutes. Besides, Nathaniel might be
up there with his guitar:

*My sweet Lord...oooh my Lord...my, my Lord...*

I hate that song.

I could go sit in the lounge and look through Buddhist
journals, except there's always a chummy little group in there
talking and laughing like mad over stuff that isn't even all that
funny.

I could just *stand* here for forty-five minutes. That would
be kind of a Zen thing to do. There's a T-shirt they sell in the
shop, it says, *Don't just do something, stand there.*

I decide to go out to my car and get this pair of work gloves
I keep in the trunk, in case I'm raking leaves again—this
morning gave me a blister on my thumb. It's a good hike to the
parking lot, on the far edge of the grounds, and as I walk along
I work on my koan:

*Just enough...just enough...just enough...*

I find the keys where I left them, under the driver's seat, but instead of going to the trunk for my gloves I sit there behind the wheel. If I wanted to, I could close the door, put the key in the ignition, drive away and be at Mom's by tomorrow evening, take a long hot shower, get into fresh clean clothes, go to this bar called the Cavern, drink a few cold ones, look around for someone sitting by her lonesome:

—*Buy you a drink?*
—*Sure.*
—*Come here a lot?*
—*Enough.*
—*Just enough?*
—*You could say. What about you?*
—*Not lately. Been in a Zen Buddhist monastery.*
—*Yeah, right.*
—*Seriously.*
—*So what're you doing here?*
—*Talking to a very attractive lady.*
—*You're pretty smooth for a monk.*
—*Ex-monk.*

Something startles me, sounded like a horse blowing through its lips like they do—Jesus, it *is* a horse. There's a wire fence just beyond the parking area with a field of grass on the other side, and this huge brown horse is standing there looking at me—hopefully, it seems.

I pocket the keys and go to him. He nods his head as I approach, like saying *That's it, attaboy.* I step up and cautiously put out my hand to touch his long face—but he blows through his lips again and I jump back, then he does too.

'Scared me,' I explain, and step up again.

So does he.

Carefully I stroke his face, telling him how nice he is, big old sad-looking thing. I wish I had an apple. I promise to bring him one tomorrow. I promise I'll visit every day around this time and bring him an apple or a carrot, *something.* I pat his massive neck. Big old fella...big old sad lonely fella...

There's tears in my eyes.

I stay with him until I hear the bell for afternoon Work Practice, pretty in the distance. Before leaving I put my palms together and bow to him.

He nods.

I get all the way back to the main building before I remember my damn gloves.

**timmy**

I wanted a horse when I was small, preferably a golden palomino with white ankles, like Gene Autry's Champion, but a spotted pinto would also be acceptable, or even a plain old brown one. But a horse of any kind or color was out of the question, given where we lived.

So I wanted a *dog* at least. But Mom pointed out he'd be covering the backyard with his business. I played back there a lot, throwing pop-ups to myself, sometimes having to dive to make the game-saving catch.

I could have a cat. But cats were snobs.

I considered a pair of hamsters, but the way they raced in those wheels—they seemed deranged.

A canary wouldn't be much more than a live decoration.

Same with a goldfish.

A turtle, though.

I bought myself one of those little dimestore jobs with racing stripes along the neck and kept him on my dresser in a bowl of shallow water with some rocks. I called him Timmy and tried to get something going between us. But he didn't even seem to know I was there. Sometimes I would hold him up in my palm in front of my face so he could have a look at his friendly owner. 'Well, *hey* there, little buddy,' I'd say to him. But he would just draw his head back into his shell.

Then one day I came in and found him standing up against the inside of the bowl, clawing away like mad, trying to climb out and escape. I thought, *Fine, if that's the way you feel. If living with me is so horrible, fine.* I took him out of the bowl and into the backyard and set him down in the middle of the lawn.

'Lotsa luck, Timmy boy,' I told him, and went in the house.

I heard a crow, and ran back out.

We got along better after that. I quit thinking of him as Timmy. He was just this turtle I happened to own along with my other stuff, my first baseman's glove, my jackknife, my binoculars. He still kept trying to escape but that was all right. I no longer took it personally.

Which seems to be the key with a lot of things.

## homesick

Raking again, we're spread out when we start—quiet, working away like good little Buddhists—but we keep moving closer, still raking but talking now too.

Nathaniel says when he gets home he's going to frame the Zen painting he did in art class, with a title: *Unleashed*.

Razor says he would be very interested in seeing the credentials of this Teacher person.

'Seems awfully full of himself for someone supposedly Zen,' I add.

Nathaniel wants to know if we would care to hear the sound of one hand clapping.

Razor stops raking. 'Yes,' he says. 'Please. By all means. Let us hear.'

Nathaniel stands at attention, rake in his left hand, and lets out a long breath. Then he closes his eyes and begins sweeping his right arm, openhanded, back and forth. 'Hear that?'

Razor sighs and returns to raking.

'What about you, Bopper?'

'Sorry.'

'You guys don't know what you're missing.'

The thing I find interesting about Nathaniel, he seems completely confident about getting his money's worth here and attaining enlightenment before our month is up. Sitting across from me at supper the other night he was saying how he'll probably just do a lot of walking around at first: 'To get my bearings, y'know? Get used to being in a state of total fucking bliss.'

'Beautiful,' he says now, eyes closed, one-hand-clapping.

'You are unwell,' Razor tells him.

When Nathaniel finishes one-hand-clapping I tell them about that horse down there by the parking lot, other side of the fence. 'There's a little...horse yard there.'

'Corral,' Razor corrects.

'And there's this *horse*, this big old brown horse, all by himself, just...all by himself in there.'

Nathaniel says, 'Yeah? So?'

'I'm just saying, think how *long* the day must be for him, you know? Just standing there? All alone? All day?'

'How do *you* know he's alone all day?'

'I could see it in his eyes.'

'See what?'

'Loneliness.'

'You should've asked him, 'Why the long face, man?''

'Yeah, that's very good, very original.'

Razor says to me, 'I am afraid you are guilty of being rather anthropomorphic.'

'Rather what?'

'Ascribing human characteristics to a nonhuman creature,' he explains.

This guy.

I tell him, 'You know what, Razor? No offense, okay? But sometimes? I think *you're* a fucking nonhuman creature.'

Nathaniel laughs loud and high.

'Please explain,' Razor says, looking more hurt than anything else.

I tell him I didn't mean it. 'You're human,' I tell him.

He gives his head a sarcastic wag. 'I am very relieved to hear it.'

Nathaniel says his dog Abigail is *totally* human, especially the way she cries, especially when he's leaving. 'By now she probably thinks I've *abandoned* her.' He looks like *he* might start crying.

Razor says his beautiful young wife Amita writes to him every day. He says you can see where the tears have fallen on the paper and smeared the ink.

I wonder if Meredith ever misses me, just a little.

We stand there holding our rakes. We could all three of us probably do with a good cry.

'Excuse me.'

It's Genzo the monk, arms at his sides. No one saw or heard him coming. These monks are like cats. 'You need to understand,' he tells us. 'This is not a time for working *and* for visiting. There *is* a time for visiting, and then we do that, wholeheartedly. But this is a time for working, for raking leaves. So that's what you need to be doing, wholeheartedly. Do you see?'

We tell him yes, we do, we see.

He bows to us.

We bow to him.

He walks away.

We rake leaves.

## meredith

It was mostly sex, what we had.

But that's a lot.

The exciting thing about Meredith, she had this old-fashioned pornographic attitude: sex was *naughty*. Before she moved in with me we used to talk on the phone a lot:

—*What are you wearing?*

—*Not a stitch.*

That sort of thing.

And in the bedroom she would get all *Catholic*. She grew up under nuns, same as me, and while we got undressed she'd be saying, 'Bopper, we mustn't, we *mustn't*.'

And I'd be saying, 'We must, Meredith. You know we must.'

'But Our *Lord* is watching.'

'He *likes* to watch.'

'Oh my God, are you...*Satan?*'

'Son of,' I would say, and drop my pants.

Then she would bring her hands to her cheeks: 'Oh Bopper, what a whopper!'

We had fun.

Outside of sex, though, we didn't have much to say. We watched a lot of really shitty TV together. Then all of a sudden out of the blue she wanted to start taking tennis lessons.

See, I think she'd already met this guy Lance somewhere. I found a business card in an empty drawer after she moved out: *Learn the Zen of tennis from a Master*, with his home phone scribbled on the back—which doesn't prove *when* he gave it to her, but I do know this: Even before she started taking 'lessons', sex between us stopped being sinful and forbidden, stopped being fun. It was now this totally wholesome, totally

natural thing. 'Life-affirming,' she called it.
I knew something was up.

**the way to rake**

If you rake angrily, thinking about things that make you angry, the tines are likely to grip too deep, they'll catch, you'll be tugging up dirt and grass, it's hard on your arms, which makes you angrier, causing you to rake even deeper, tugging up even more dirt and grass, until you're wondering once again what the fuck you're doing here.

On the other hand, if you rake like Nathaniel—walking steadily backwards, dragging the rake along, barely skimming the grass, quietly singing an old Mamas and Papas song about all the leaves being brown and the sky being gray, you're not going to get very many leaves, but you probably don't especially care.

But if you rake like *Razor*—brushing gently but firmly at the grass with a steady rhythm—then you get all the leaves and only leaves, the grass left behind is perfectly clean, your wife is very beautiful, your life is deeply satisfying, and your shit doesn't stink.

MEDITATION

**jordan**

This older guy Jordan—I'm pretty sure that's his name—is sitting next to me in the dining hall, where we're all waiting in our robes to go upstairs to the Zendo for afternoon meditation. I don't know how long he's been at the monastery, pretty long I think, but he's not a monk—he has his hair and his real name. He's a very quiet guy, does a lot of writing in a notebook. That's what he was doing just now, but somehow he must have picked up on the way I'm feeling—tired, discouraged, depressed—and leans his head near mine. 'It's very hard here,' he whispers. 'We sit and sit and nothing comes of it. We want something to happen, but nothing does. We go on, though. And then one day, when we're not even looking for it anymore, when we're just sitting there—something happens.'

I nod.

'Give up,' he says.

I look at him.

'But don't quit,' he adds, and returns to his notebook.

## possibly samadhi

I start the sitting period with lots of energy and determination. I can do this. I just have to stay with it. *Don't quit*, Jordan said. And I'm going pretty good, staying with the breath...staying with the breath. Then Nathaniel begins placing a neon yellow lemon drop smack in the middle of my brain. I try very hard to ignore it, silently counting *one* on the inhalation, then pushing out hard on the exhalation, *twoooo...*

It's not working. This *place* is not working. It's just not. I've tried, I really have. That guy Jordan said to give up but don't quit. Well, I give up *and* I quit, as of now, right after this sitting period. When we get up to do walking meditation—kinhin— I'm going to kinhin right on out of here. I mean it. I'm through. It's been interesting, something to talk about: *I once stayed for a week in a Zen Buddhist monastery...*

I sit there, lemon drops coming and going.

I sit there.

Just sit there.

Just sit...

The little bell gives a ding and I return to the surface.

Wow.

Where have I been?

In samadhi?

I was definitely down there in *something* and I think it might have been samadhi, I really do. *Body and mind fallen away*, that's how the books describe it, and that's how it was. I can't even say for how long—how *could* I say?

Samadhi.

This is encouraging. This is very encouraging.

*Ding*, the bell for kinhin.

Stepping along behind Razor, up one row of mats and down the other, I can't help feeling excited, like I'm finally starting to make some actual *progress* here. Out there earlier raking leaves I had those five astounding here-and-now seconds, and now *this*, a little taste of samadhi.

But I try to forget about it. I try to let it go, just focus on my walking, on the cool floor beneath my bare feet and so on, because you're not supposed to be trying to make progress, trying to get somewhere. There's nowhere to get. There's only here, this very moment, this very breath, like what we're doing now, doing kinhin: not walking to *arrive* somewhere, just walking.

It's hard, though. It's very hard to stop caring about making progress. But you *have* to stop caring if you want to make any real progress.

We're walking now along the row towards the head monk Shugen who's sitting on his cushion, in full lotus, observing us. As I approach I'm telling myself, *Don't do the phony face, don't do the scowl, don't do it...*

And I don't. I walk past him wearing whatever face I happen to be wearing, I couldn't tell you. So: another achievement to try and not feel pleased about.

**quick zen story**

When the great sage Bodhidharma met the Chinese emperor, the emperor told him about the many Buddhist temples he'd built and the hundreds of monks he supported. Then he asked, 'What merit shall I gain?'

'No merit,' said the great sage.

This made the emperor very angry. He got up from his throne and said, 'Who is this standing before me?'

Bodhidarma laughed like hell. 'No idea, Your Majesty!'

**a new sound**

We're about halfway through the second sitting period and it's going good, *very* good in fact. I'm letting Nathaniel suck on his lemon drops, not a serious problem, and whenever I happen to catch myself drifting off on a thought, about lemon drops or anything else, I let go of it like the string of a balloon and drop back down to where I'm sitting, right here, right now, and every time I return I feel even *more* right here and now. So this is good, this is very encouraging, and of course I'm letting go of *that* balloon too.

Then Nathaniel starts making a brand new sound: *'Kuh... kuh...'*

I sneak a look. He's sitting there with his mouth open, eyes bugging out: *'Kuh... kuh...'*

Oh God, oh fuck.

*'Kuh...'*

I turn to Razor and poke his arm.

'Why are you striking me?' he whispers.

'He's choking.'

'Who is choking?'

'Nathaniel. Help him. Hurry.'

Razor gets up, goes over and kneels behind him, wraps him in his arms, gives a hard jerk, and a lemon drop flies from Nathaniel's mouth, landing behind Rachel, my dishwashing partner, who frowns over her shoulder.

The moderator, this giant monk named Yokan, comes loping over on his big red feet. Nathaniel is still sitting there in half lotus, a wild look in his eye, Razor standing over him, palms together, mission accomplished.

'Are you all right?' Yokan whispers, but Nathaniel just keeps staring off, so he turns to Razor. 'What happened?'

Razor gives one of his little head-wags: 'He was choking.'

'On *that*,' Rachel whispers, pointing at the lemon drop on the floor.

Yokan helps Nathaniel to his feet and walks him out of the Zendo, Razor returning to his cushion. A little monk I've never seen before appears with a hand broom and dustpan, sweeps up the lemon drop, and hurries off.

All is quiet once again.

### the heimlich maneuver

Mr. Brogan showed us how in gym one day, using this fat kid David Norling, who farted when he was squeezed and we all laughed, even Mr. Brogan a little. Then he paired us up and told us to take turns. Everyone was embarrassed, putting our arms around another guy, and tried to make a joke of it, but Mr. Brogan threatened us with push-ups and we settled down. He went around observing, correcting, and we learned how to do it. I still remember how. I could have done what Razor did. I could have done it easily.

LIGHT SUPPER

### nathaniel's speck of light

Sitting across from me at supper, he won't shut up. For a full twenty seconds he was staring straight into the Void, he says. It was very dark out there, he says, but he thinks he may have seen something: a light.

'Then it wasn't a void,' I tell him. I shouldn't have sat here.

'Way far off in the distance,' he says, looking way far off: 'a speck of light.'

Someone at the table wants to know if he was in a tunnel.

'Actually, like a...more like a...'

'Sea of infinite emptiness?' someone else offers.

'*Kind* of, but with this tiny speck of light, way far off, like there was someone out there holding up a...some kind of a...'

'Flashlight? He lost his,' I tell the others. 'It's probably on the floor under all his—'

'More like a *lantern*,' he says.

'Ah,' from someone.

They're only humoring him. Serious Zen students don't do a lot of pondering on the afterlife: just another distraction.

'Someone was definitely out there holding up a lantern,' Nathaniel says. 'They were trying to show me the way.'

'You should eat,' a woman tells him.

He lifts a spoonful of mushroom soup towards his mouth, but then he lowers it: 'Razor saved my life.'

I don't want to hear this.

'If it wasn't for Razor,' he says, looking off again, 'I'd be out there right now, trying to get to that light.'

I do not want to hear this.

'Out there *crawling* towards it, on my hands and—'

'I told you be*fore*,' I say to him, getting up with my tray,

103

people looking but I don't care. 'You have no business sucking lemon drops in the Zendo—I *told* you that, jerk-off.'

Nathaniel looks up at me with a sweet, forgiving smile.

## when the hands clap

There's an hour before evening meditation and I get my coat from the dressing room behind the cafeteria and go out for a walk around the grounds. It's already dark out but I've got my flashlight.

*Fuck.*

You know?

You start thinking you're finally making some progress, finally actually getting somewhere, then something like this happens. *If it wasn't for Razor,* he said, and he's right, if it wasn't for Razor he'd be dead. I knew what to do—like I said, we learned in gym—but I froze. I had to get Razor, who didn't even hesitate.

*When the hands clap, the sound does not wait to come forth.*

That's a Zen saying. It means you don't sit there going *Oh God, oh fuck.* You react like Razor did—immediately, without *over*reacting.

Just enough.

It was a test. You know? A test of my Zenhood. Which I flunked. Miserably.

I start heading in the direction of the parking lot, walking faster. This place just keeps making me feel like a fucking failure.

When I get to my car, as I'm opening the door, that horse starts blowing through his lips in the dark, letting me know he's there, hoping for a visit, maybe even an apple or a carrot like I promised him.

*'I'm sorry,'* I shout. *'I don't have anything. Nothing. I'm sorry!'*

I get in the car, wipe my eyes with my coat sleeve, and start driving home.

**my car**

You should see this thing, a big old Chevy Bonneville. It was my mom's. I gave her a token hundred dollars for it when she bought her coupe. I keep it filthy dirty to hide the pretty, mint-green color, and took the hubcaps off, which also helps. Plus it needs a new muffler, so it not only looks but *sounds* ugly. And if you concentrate you can still get a slight whiff of the beer I spilled on the front seat over a year ago.

I'm saying I like this car, the attitude it gives me. Sitting behind the wheel, I feel like I'm this guy who just plain doesn't give a shit, this carefree guy they call *Bopper*.

## collect

Even so, even though I'm this carefree guy they call Bopper, I pull into an empty little mall in a town just a couple of miles away, where there's a telephone booth. I've still got Lance's business card I found in Meredith's drawer, with his home phone on the back. I just hope *she* answers.

She does.

'I have a collect call to Meredith from Bopper,' the operator says to her. 'Will you accept the charge?'

She gives a weary sigh: 'Yes, operator.'

'Go ahead, caller.'

'Hi. Listen, send me the bill for this, okay? To my mom's. I'll give you the address. It's—'

'Why are you calling here, Bopper?'

That was pretty cold. I wasn't quite ready for that. 'Well, I just...thought I'd just...you know...'

'Hang on a second. Be right back.' She bangs the phone down.

The truth is, the reason I'm calling—collect—is so she'll get a bill that proves where I've been: somewhere out in the Catskill Mountains, at a Zen monastery, meditating in a robe, reciting chants, raking leaves, eating tofu.

'All right,' she says, 'I'm back.'

'Problem?' I ask.

'I had to let the cat in.'

'You have a cat?'

'What is it you wanted, Bopper?'

'You hate cats.'

'No. Cats are sacred.'

'What, according to Lance?'

107

'Bopper, is there some reason—'

'Funny, y'know? I've never even met the guy.'

'—some particular reason you're calling?'

'I always picture him in a suit of armor—Sir *Lancelot*, right?'

'Because otherwise I'm afraid I'm going to have to—'

'Me, I don't *wear* any armor. No protection. Nothing between me and—'

'Are you in a bar somewhere?'

'I'll *tell* you where I am—where I've *been* anyway—at a Zen Buddhist monastery, Meredith, okay? Has *Lance* ever been to one? Just curious.'

'You're drunk.'

I kind of *feel* like it. 'How *is* the old boy, by the way.'

'Fine. He's gone to pick up some Chinese. He'll be back any minute. So if you don't mind—'

'Do you like tofu? They serve a lot of that at the Zen monastery, the one where I was staying. No meat of course, mostly vegetables. They grow their own. The head gardener's an old woman named Hojin. Wonderful lady. *Her* idea of sacred is when her radishes come up. 'Striving towards the light' she calls it.'

'Are you...*on* something?'

'I like that, 'Striving towards the light'.'

'I'm going to hang up now, Bopper.'

'I had a naughty dream about you last night.'

She's quiet for a moment. 'Oh?' she says.

'Dancing for me, in just your little tennis skirt.'

'What, the pleated one?'

'Real slow and snaky. Plus you had your racket, running your hand up and down the...what's it called...'

'The shaft?'

'There you go. Up and down the shaft, Meredith.'

'Slowly, you mean?'

'Very slowly.'

I mentioned earlier, we used to do this, talk dirty over the phone like this. Sounds to me like she misses it. I imagine life-affirming sex can get kind of boring after a while.

'So,' she says, just wondering, 'were you…*enjoying* my little dance?'

'Are you kidding?'

'Did it get you…hard?'

'Are you kidding?'

'Are you hard right now?'

'Hard isn't the word for it.'

Actually, *limp* is the word for it, because all of a sudden this is depressing, standing here in a phone booth in a dark deserted parking lot talking dirty to someone else's girlfriend eight hundred miles away.

She wants to know what happened *then?* 'I was dancing, you were hard—then what? Tell me. Hurry.'

Evening meditation will be starting soon. I picture my cushion, my zafu, between Razor and Nathaniel, with nobody on it: *Looks like Bopper couldn't take it*, they'll be thinking. *When the going got tough, he got going—straight home.*

'Bopper?' says Meredith, all worked up now, breathing kind of fast. 'You still there?'

'Yeah.'

'So *then* what? Tell me. Let's hear.'

'Then I woke up. Listen, send me the bill for this.' I give her the name and address of the monastery. 'I forget the zip, you'll have to look it up.'

'So you really *are* at a Zen monastery?'

'Send me the bill.'

As I drive on back, the moon looks like a slice of ripe cantaloupe. Maybe we'll have some for breakfast tomorrow. That would be nice.

## cantaloupe à la mode

I've always had a thing for cantaloupe.

I'll never forget—I think it was for my birthday—Mom served me an entire half a cantaloupe, with a ball of vanilla ice cream in the scooped-out center. It looked very pretty but I wasn't sure how well it would work. I had never heard of such a combination. I liked ice cream, and of course cantaloupe, but the two of them together like this—I just wasn't sure. Mom was always making odd combinations, trying to be creative, and a lot of them worked out badly, pineapple wedges in the spaghetti sauce, for example. But while she stood there waiting, I went ahead and ran the edge of the spoon to get a sliver of cantaloupe onto it, then stabbed up a dab of ice cream on top, and brought the spoon to my mouth.

I almost burst out crying, that's how incredibly delicious it was.

'Well?' she said.

I held up my thumb and kept eating.

Then Mom actually *did* start crying, or anyway had tears in her eyes. She was always very tearful back then, I remember. 'We're going to be fine, Bopper, do you know that?' she said, running her arm across her eyes. 'We're going to be just fine.'

Who ever said we weren't?

MEDITATION/DOKUSAN

**why did the chicken cross the road?**

About five minutes into evening meditation Shugen at the back of the Zendo breaks the silence: 'Stop showing off.'

I'm sure he means Nathaniel, who's sitting next to me holding his upturned palms in the air like a Hindu holy man. He drops them back in his lap where they belong.

Then Jinmon announces, 'The dokusan line is now open to those in the far row on the south side of the Zendo.'

That's us.

I get up and run with the others—it's supposed to show how eager we are to go see the Master, but I feel silly, like a Kmart shopper at the announcement of a sale in aisle three. Razor gets there first, then Nathaniel, then me, then the rest of the row, all of us kneeling in a line along the back of the hall, one behind the other. When you're about to be next, you move up and kneel in front of this stone bell and wait there with a wooden mallet. When you hear the Master's little bell, you hit yours to let him know, then get up and go to his room—the Dharma Room, it's called. Kneeling there in line, waiting my turn, I'm trying to think what to ask him.

—*Why did the chicken cross the road?*

Which actually isn't such a bad question. Why *did* he cross the road? To get to the other side, sure, but what was he looking for? What was he hoping to find? Did he ever find it?

The bell from the Dharma Room rings, *ching-ching*, and out comes Razor, palms together, returning to his cushion. Meanwhile, Nathaniel ahead of me taps the stone bell, *bong*, then gets up and goes to see the Master. I take his place by the bell: on my knees, mallet ready.

I think what I'll do when I go in there, I'll just wing it, just go in and walk up, kneel down, open my mouth and see what comes out. You never know what's down there—*who's* down there. You might *think* you know, but then who's the one thinking you know? How does that quote go again? *Seeking the mind with the mind...*

*Ching-ching*, from the Dharma Room.

That was quick.

I tap the bell and set down the mallet. Then I yank my robe off my heels, get to my feet and go along the short hallway. Just before I get to the door it opens and Nathaniel comes marching out, all red-faced. 'Fuck this place,' he says, shoving past me. Then instead of returning to the Zendo he stomps over to the shoe racks, grabs his boots and socks, and without even pausing to put them on he heads down the stairwell leading outside.

He's quitting. He's leaving. Heading back to Surf City. Good. I'm glad. No more fucking lemon drops. I step into the Dharma Room and close the door behind me.

The Master is sitting on the other side of the room on a small platform in his black and brown robes, like a breathing brick wall, legs crossed under him, eyes lowered, hands cupped in his lap. I give a low bow and go over there holding my palms together, kneel down, give a short bow, sit back on my heels, and look at him. His eyes are still lowered, his mouth turned down. He looks fierce. I wonder what Nathaniel said to get quick-belled like that. I recite the introductory bit: 'My name is Bopper and my practice is counting the breath.'

And that's it. That's all I've got. I wait for more, but nothing comes. I sit there like an idiot.

The Abbot lifts his eyes and looks at me.

Words come tumbling out of my mouth: 'Master, that guy that was just here—Nathaniel?—I think he's gonna quit, in fact I'm sure of it, he said something just now to that effect and he didn't go back in the Zendo. I'm pretty sure he's heading up to the cabin to get his stuff and go home. He's a very aggravating person, as I'm sure you probably noticed, but it seems a shame, you know? Him leaving like this? He came here on a *bus*, Master. That's what he told me. He's from California and came all the way out here on a bus, afraid of flying. So now he's probably going all the way *back* on one, sitting there staring out the window. So I was thinking maybe you could send one of the monks up there, you know? See if they could talk to him?'

'You go,' he says, and rings his bell.

## bodhisattva

I'm not calling myself a bodhisattva. That would be pure ego, which a true bodhisattva is completely free of, the original bodhisattva choosing to put off his final enlightenment until he helped everyone else arrive. That's the kind of person he was. Which I'm not in any way comparing myself to, believe me. True, I did speak to the Abbot about *Nathaniel's* needs instead of my own, which is exactly the kind of thing a bodhisattva would do, but calling myself therefore some kind of bodhisattva, that's pretty ridiculous.

I mean, come on.

## nathaniel

Nearing the top of the hill I can already hear him slapping away at his guitar, shouting more than singing: *'I really wanna see you, really wanna be with you...'*

I hate that song, I think I mentioned.

*'But it takes so long, my Lord...'*

I stand in the doorway behind my flashlight and he stops, looking scared: 'Who *is* it?' he says.

I shine the light on my face.

'Oh.'

I step into the cabin. 'Who'd you think it was, your friend with the lantern?'

'Fuck you,' he says without much energy, sitting on the edge of the bed in his meditation robe, guitar across his lap. His face is red and wet. There's a bulging duffel bag leaning next to him. 'Get that off-a me, will ya?'

I turn off the flashlight. There's enough moonlight in the room.

He asks me what I'm doing here in my robe.

I ask him what he's doing here in his.

He starts tuning the guitar, turning knobs, thumbing different strings.

'You taking off?' I ask him.

He keeps tuning the guitar.

I ask him what happened back there. 'The Abbot yell at you or something?'

'Fuck no, I yelled at *him*. The guy's an asshole.'

'What'd he do?'

He quits dicking around with the guitar and gives a sigh. 'I go in there, okay? Start telling him about my...you know...'

'Your vision?'

'Trying to describe it: little old skinny Chinese guy in a black robe and sandals, lousy teeth, long gray hair and beard…'

'Sounds like the art teacher.'

'I'm telling you what I *saw*, okay? Sitting in the Zendo tonight. I got *into* it, man. I was seeing him really clear: holding up a lantern with this little smile on his face. Then fuckin' Shugen hollers at me.'

"Stop showing off"?'

'I wasn't showing *off*, man. I was *into* it.'

'All right. So what happened with the Abbot?'

Another big sigh. 'So I'm telling him about it, right? What it was *like* out there, in the Void, crawling towards the light, all that. And here's what he says: 'Drop it.' Just like that. 'Drop it,' he says. I go, 'Excuse me?' Then he just sits there giving me the hairy eyeball. I try again, 'E*xcuse* me?' So then he rings his little chickenshit bell. I told him, 'Fine, fuck this place'.'

'You said that?'

'Something like that.'

'So now you're going home.'

He shrugs.

'You won't get a refund,' I remind him.

Another shrug.

All of a sudden I'm very, very tired. 'Move over,' I tell him. He scoots over and I sit next to him. We sit there. After a minute I tell him, 'I started heading home tonight my*self*.'

He looks at me.

'I got as far as that first little town. What's it called?'

'Fishkill?'

'That's it.'

'So what made you turn around?'

'Basically? You and Razor.'

He moves away a little. 'How do you mean?'

'I didn't want you fuckers calling me a quitter.'

'Oh.'

We sit there.

'So…that's what you'd be calling *me*?'

'Bet your ass,' I tell him.

We sit there.

He shakes his head. 'Man…'

'What.'

'I thought this place would be a lot different, y'know? A lot more…I don't know…'

'Interesting?'

'People *levitating*, shit like that. It's fucking *boring* here, man.' He shakes his head again. 'I prob'ly should've read more about Zen before I decided.'

'I probably should've read less.'

We sit there some more.

I decide to clear the air about something. 'By the way, just for the record, I meant to try and save you, okay?'

He looks at me.

'In the Zendo, when you were choking,' I explain. 'I meant to try and, you know, help you out.'

'But what, you were busy?'

'I froze, okay? I knew what to do, I know how to do that maneuver. But I froze. I had to get Razor.'

'Yeah, well…you did *that* anyway.'

'I know, but see, the *Zen* reaction would have been to—'

'Fuck the Zen reaction,' he says. 'Fuck Zen. I'm sick of Zen.'

I am too, I realize.

We sit there, sick of Zen.

'I just wish you picked someone else instead of Razor,' he says. 'I hate being grateful to *that* fucking guy.'

'Don't worry, he thinks everyone should be grateful to him.'

'Right, just for being *among* us.'

'For speaking to us.'

'*Breathing* with us.'

We sit there hating Razor.

'Anyway,' I tell him, 'that's a very scary experience, choking like that. I almost choked on a chunk of melon yesterday morning, so I know.'

He turns to me. 'Wait. Was that when you stood up and spread out your arms? I've been wanting to ask you about that. Is that what you were doing? Choking?'

'That's what I was doing.'

He gives a laugh. 'I thought you were gonna *say* something, man. The way you stood up and spread out your arms, I thought you had some kind of *message*.'

'It was just the cantaloupe.'

'Some kind of revel*ation*.'

'I was just trying to swallow.'

'Then you sat back down and I thought maybe it was supposed to be some kind of silent *Zen* message, you know?'

'Just the cantaloupe.'

We sit there.

'So,' he says, 'did you...you know...'

'What.'

'See anything?'

'How do you mean?'

'While you were choking, y'know? Close to death? On the threshold? All that? Happen to see anything?'

'A Chinaman with a lantern for instance?'

'Or whatever. *Any*thing?'

'I saw myself dropping dead in front of everyone like a fucking fool.'

'That was it?'

'I didn't see squat.'

We sit there.

'Me neither,' he says.

I look at him.

'I just made that shit up,' he says.

'What, the whole thing? About the Chinaman?'

'Hey, it *could* be true. I'm pretty sure I saw *something*. It *coulda* been a Chinaman holding up a lantern.'

'It coulda been Ronald McDonald holding up a cheeseburger.'

'That's what I'm *saying*, man.'

I can't get over it. 'You made that whole thing up?'

'Listen, by the time I went to see the Abbot, I *believed* in that fucking Chinaman. He was showing me the way, *encouraging* me, like Teacher this morning. I *need* that shit. I didn't think I did, but I do.'

'And then the Abbot tells you to drop it.'

'Then he just sits there looking at me.' He shakes his head. 'I hate the fuckin' way he looks at me.'

'I know what you mean.'

'It's like...I don't know...'

'Nowhere to hide?'

He nods. 'Right,' he says quietly.

We sit there, nowhere to hide.

After a minute, hands on my knees, I push myself to my feet. 'Come on. Evening service.'

He keeps sitting there, staring ahead.

'You don't need any fucking Chinaman,' I tell him.

He goes on sitting there.

'He wants you to come back, okay?'

He looks at me. 'The Chinaman?'

'The *Abbot*. He told me to come and get you.'

'Seriously?'

'What the hell do you think I'm doing here?'

'I was wondering, man.'

'Come on. I hate walking in late.'

'Yeah, well...I hope he's not expecting an apology.'

'I doubt it.'

'I'll accept one from *him*, if *that's* why he wants to see me.'

'I don't think he wants to see you, he just wants you to, you know, return to the fold.'

'Fine. I don't mind. Anything to make the great fuckin'

*Master* happy.' He lays his guitar in its case behind him on the bed. 'Look what I found under my stuff,' he says, and holds it up: his flashlight.

I'm very glad and tell him so.


Heading back down the hill, Nathaniel leads the way, talking all about his dog Abigail, how smart she is, and affectionate, and how much he misses her.

EVENING SERVICE

## hula

Shugen closes the service by chanting alone, palms together, elbows out:

*'Let me respectfully remind you,*
*Life and death are of supreme importance.*
*Time swiftly passes and opportunity is lost.*
*Each of us must strive to awaken…awaken.*
*Take heed: do not squander your liiife.'*

Afterwards, heading up the hill again, well behind Nathaniel, I wonder if I'm squandering my life, or as Shugen puts it, my *liiife*, like falling off a cliff, like there goes your life. I decide I'm probably not squandering it *here* anyway, since they're the ones telling me not to squander it. But what about after I'm out? I'll be out of here in three weeks. What about then?

I don't know.

Maybe by that time I'll attain enlightenment and not have to worry: walking around all serene and cheerful, smiling at everyone, even Jerry. I try it out, nodding and smiling at the darkness on either side of the path, holding up my thumb. Then I trip, stumble and come down hard on the same fucking knee as this morning.

And while I'm kneeling there waiting for the pain to pass, that picture all of a sudden comes to me, full on: Mom hula-dancing for Jerry in the kitchen. It's a picture I usually manage to switch off the moment it appears, but now I look at it, look at *her*. She's moving smoothly, stepping back and forth in her bare feet, swaying her grass-skirted hips, using her arms in the wavy way they do, eyes closed, this dreamy little smile on her face. She's enjoying herself. She's *happy*.

For Christ sake, leave her be.

**razor**

I'm getting to my feet when Razor comes up behind. 'Are you injured?'

'I'm okay. I tripped and fell.'

'Sometimes it is good to fall,' he informs me, always the guru. We head up the hill, me in front.

'As a boy,' he says, 'I once fell from a tree in our yard.'

'And was it good to fall?'

'I sprained my ankle.'

'Ah, that's painful. I've done that.'

'Here is the manner in which I wept,' he says, and lets out this long, low, horrible, heartbroken moan.

When he's finally through I ask him, 'You okay back there?'

No reply.

'Razor?'

'And *your* sprained ankle?' he says. 'How did yours occur?'

'Playing baseball,' I tell him. 'Do you know baseball at all?'

'Somewhat.'

'I was sliding into second base and my spike shoe caught in the dirt. Jesus, was I in pain.'

'Not as *I* was,' he says.

'Well, no,' I admit. 'You sounded like a…like some kind of…'

'Soul in torment?'

'Sort of.' More like a *dog* in torment, I was thinking but didn't say.

We're quiet then for a couple of minutes, climbing.

Then he surprises me: 'I am very tired, Bopper,' he says.

I can tell he doesn't mean just physically. 'Me too, Razor,' I tell him. 'Me too.'

'Not as *I* am,' he says.

'Well, no, of course not.'
We're quiet the rest of the way up.

LIGHTS OUT

**cricket**

It's late. I'm still awake, lying on my back staring up at the dark. Razor on my left is snoring, soft and low. Nathaniel on my right mutters something in his sleep. Somewhere in the cabin there's a cricket singing, wholeheartedly:

*Tonight I'm fine...*
*Tonight I'm fine...*
*Tonight I'm fine...*
That's a good little song.